LOVE MORE

The Journal Edition

April Maria Williams, Esq.
& Crystal Dionne Williams

JumpTime Publishing

Copyright © 2022 April Maria Williams,
Esq & Crystal Dionne Williams

All rights reserved

The characters and events portrayed in this book are fictitious. Any similarity to real persons, living or dead, is coincidental and not intended by the author.

No part of this book may be reproduced, or stored in a retrieval system, or transmitted in any form or by any means, electronic, mechanical, photocopying, recording, or otherwise, without express written permission of the publisher.

ISBN-13: 978-1-7378595-5-0

*This book is dedicated to those
that want to Love More!*

Love More was created to celebrate Love. We need to tell each other that we love one another more often. In a time where hate, separation and cancel culture is at an all-time high, make the decision to **Love More**!

How To Use This Book?

This book was written in a journal format. It is recommended that you read the text of each chapter. Take a moment to reflect on the chapter text. Then go to the journal portion and answer the questions based on your reflections and thoughts.

LOVE IS LIFE

Love gives us life. Love is in the air that we breathe. Love is life changing. God gives us life so that we can love.

If you want to **Love More**, know that Love is life.

Love Is Life: The Journal Edition

When was the last time you felt a love that gave you life?

Have you ever felt a love that was life changing?

What are you going to do to love in life more?

LOVE MORE

LOVE IS NEEDED

Love is needed by everyone on the earth. When we love, we feel good about ourselves and the people around us. Love is needed to make the world go around.

If you want to **Love More**, know that Love is needed from us all.

Love Is Needed: The Journal Edition

Can you recall a time where you felt you needed love or where love was needed from you?

How are you going to give love when it is needed?

LOVE MORE

_____

_____

_____

_____

_____

LOVE IS WANTED

Love is wanted by us all. We all want to be loved by someone. Whether it's from our families, friends, or those we are in relationships with, we all want to be loved. Love wants us just as much as we want it!

If you want to **Love More**, know that your Love is wanted.

Love Is Wanted: The Journal Edition

When was the last time you felt that your love was not wanted?

_____

_____

_____

_____

_____

_____

_____

_____

_____

_____

_____

_____

_____

_____

Do you know that no matter what, your love is wanted by someone known or unknown?

LOVE MORE

LOVE IS EASY

Love should be an easy part of life, but it can be difficult to maintain. Love can be easy if we learn to be genuine and true to ourselves and others. Love can be easy if we understand that no one is perfect.

If you want to **Love More**, know that Love is easy.

Love Is Easy: The Journal Edition

When was the last time you felt love was not easy?

_____

_____

_____

_____

_____

_____

_____

_____

_____

_____

_____

_____

_____

_____

_____

_____

_____

How did you work through the love that was not easy?

LOVE MORE

LOVE IS UNCONDITIONAL

Love is supposed to be unconditional, but today it is everything but. We put conditions on everything in life, including love. This makes it hard to love unconditionally. How would the world be if we truly loved unconditionally? No hearts broken and more relationships in full bloom. There would be less hurt because our love would be unconditional.

If you want to **Love More**, love unconditionally. Love is greater when it is unconditional.

Love Is Unconditional: The Journal Edition

Have you ever put boundaries on the love you give?

_____

_____

_____

_____

_____

_____

_____

_____

_____

_____

_____

_____

_____

Has anyone ever put boundaries on the love they gave to you? If so, how did it make you feel?

How can you work to love unconditional?

APRIL MARIA WILLIAMS, ESQ.

LOVE IS NOT BITTER

Love is not bitter. It is hard to believe that there is love when the person is bitter. Hurt, anger and fear are strong emotions that can interfere with the love you give and receive. Don't allow bitterness to taint your heart. Love and allow yourself to be loved.

If you want to **Love More**, know that love is not bitter. Don't let your past affect your love moving forward.

Love Is Not Bitter: The Journal Edition

Have you ever felt bitter about love?

_____

_____

_____

_____

_____

_____

_____

_____

_____

_____

_____

_____

_____

_____

_____

Have you moved past the bitterness?

_____

_____

_____

_____

If not, how do you plan on moving past the bitterness so that you are open to love?

_____

_____

_____

_____

_____

_____

_____

_____

_____

_____

_____

LOVE MORE

LOVE IS NOT HARD

Love is not hard. Far too often we are told that love it supposed to be hard work. Love itself is not hard. Loving is the easiest thing to do! We make love hard through our actions and inactions.

If you want to **Love More**, stop making love so hard. Love is not hard!

Love Is Not Hard: The Journal Edition

When was the last time you felt that love was hard?

_____

_____

_____

_____

_____

_____

_____

_____

_____

_____

_____

_____

_____

_____

_____

How did the hard love make you feel?

Did you realize that love was not hard?

How are you going to reform your actions to not make love hard?

LOVE MORE

_____

_____

_____

_____

_____

_____

LOVE IS NOT MONEY DRIVEN

Love is not driven by money. Love cannot be bought. There is a thought that we can buy our way to love, but you cannot buy an emotion that comes from deep within.

If you want to **Love More**, know that love is not driven by money. Love is an emotion, a feeling that comes from deep within.

Love Is Not Money Driven: The Journal Edition

Do you attach a dollar value to how much you love someone or how much they love you?

_____

_____

_____

_____

_____

_____

_____

_____

_____

_____

_____

_____

Can you love without attaching a dollar value to love?

How do you plan to love without attaching a dollar value to love?

APRIL MARIA WILLIAMS, ESQ.

LOVE IS NOT A THING

Love is not a thing that can be touched or felt with the flesh. It is something that runs deep within us. It is not an object that can be explained away. Love is so much more than just a thing.

If you want to **Love More**, know that Love is not just a thing.

Love Is Not A Thing: The Journal Edition

How can you look at love as more than just a thing?

_____

_____

_____

_____

_____

_____

_____

_____

_____

_____

_____

_____

_____

_____

_____

_____

LOVE MORE

LOVE IS EMOTION

Oftentimes, people try to take the emotion out of love. But love is an emotion. Love is a feeling. People try to remove the emotion from love, but they often fail. Accept love for what it is, an emotion.

If you want to **Love More**, understand and accept that love is an emotion.

Love Is Emotion: The Journal Edition

Have you ever tried to take emotion out of love?

_____
_____
_____
_____
_____
_____
_____
_____
_____
_____
_____
_____
_____
_____
_____

How do you plan to keep the emotion in your love?

LOVE MORE

LOVE IS BEAUTIFUL

Love is beautiful! Experiencing unconditional love is the most beautiful thing! The beauty of love is indescribable.

If you want to **Love More**, know that love is Beautiful! The beauty in love is within us all. Your love is beautiful!

Love Is Beautiful: The Journal Edition

Have you ever tried to take the beauty out of love?

_____

_____

_____

_____

_____

_____

_____

_____

_____

_____

_____

_____

_____

_____

_____

How can you remind yourself of the beauty that is love?

LOVE MORE

LOVE IS GOD

God is Love and Love is God. The Bible says love is patient, love is kind. Sometimes we forget how much God loves us and calls for us to love each other. We must remember to love as God loves us.

If you want to **Love More**, you have to remember that Love is God and to show it every day.

Love Is God: The Journal Edition

Have you ever tried to take God out of your love?

How can you remind yourself that God is Love?

LOVE MORE

ABOUT THE AUTHORS

April Maria Williams and Crystal Dionne Williams are two loving sisters that just want to make the world a better place. They have seen the good, the bad and ugly of this world and want to make their positive contribution to the world.

Love More does just that!

LOVE MORE

JUST LOVE MORE

Made in the USA
Columbia, SC
02 April 2022